Sylvester Waterhouse

A Eulogy on the Late Chancellor Joseph Gibson Hoyt of Washington University

Delivered at the Hall of the University, St. Louis, Jan. 20, 1863

Sylvester Waterhouse

A Eulogy on the Late Chancellor Joseph Gibson Hoyt of Washington University
Delivered at the Hall of the University, St. Louis, Jan. 20, 1863

ISBN/EAN: 9783337424350

Printed in Europe, USA, Canada, Australia, Japan

Cover: Foto ©Raphael Reischuk / pixelio.de

More available books at **www.hansebooks.com**

A

EULOGY

ON THE LATE

CHANCELLOR JOSEPH GIBSON HOYT

OF

WASHINGTON UNIVERSITY.

BY

PROF. S. WATERHOUSE.

Delivered at the Hall of the University, St. Louis, Jan. 20, 1863.

PHILADELPHIA:

J. B. LIPPINCOTT & CO.

1863.

A

EULOGY

ON THE LATE

CHANCELLOR JOSEPH GIBSON HOYT

OF

WASHINGTON UNIVERSITY.

BY

PROF. S. WATERHOUSE.

Delivered at the Hall of the University, St. Louis, Jan. 20, 1863.

PHILADELPHIA:

J. B. LIPPINCOTT & CO.

1863.

Washington University, Nov. 26, 1862.

Resolved, That PROF. S. WATERHOUSE be requested to prepare a eulogy on the late CHANCELLOR HOYT, to be delivered at the earliest day convenient to himself.

EULOGY.

Τοῦ μὲν γὰρ οὐδὲν ἄλγος ἅψεταί ποτε
Πολλῶν δὲ μόχθων εὐκλεὴς ἐπαύσατο.

JOSEPH GIBSON HOYT was born in Dunbarton, New Hampshire, January 19th, 1815. He was the son of Joshua F. and Olive R. Hoyt. His father was a plain farmer, who, by prudent husbandry, had acquired a competency. Of limited education, ingenuous nature, good talents, and sound judgment, he thought more of an honest life and material success than of liberal culture. That his children should lead lives of simple virtue and humble prosperity satisfied his highest aspirations. From his low estimate of the value of education, the result of his own want of culture, he was unwilling to send his son to college. He did not deem education a profitable investment. But at last the father's pride was gratified by the son's success, and help came when the youth had proved his ability to succeed without it.

But the mother was a woman of brilliant powers and marked traits of character. She was distinguished for facility of composition and a quaint originality of expression. Gifted, aspiring, energetic, and pious, she was nobly ambitious that her children

(5)

should be conspicuous for learning and public usefulness. She taught them to hate meanness and vice, to love purity and frankness, and to aspire to honorable and virtuous distinction. She impressed her own qualities upon the plastic and susceptible nature of her most gifted son, and exercised a decisive influence in the formation of his character.

The subject of this memoir was the second of nine children. In childhood, the charms of personal beauty rendered his artless manners still more attractive. His complexion was fair, his features finely chiseled, curling locks fell in golden masses around his brow, and his deep-blue eye had a sweet and tender beauty that is still remembered.

In his earliest years, Joseph Gibson was noted for quickness of apprehension. Nothing pleased him more than the printed page. He would gaze with astonished delight upon the mysterious characters, and try to decipher their hidden meaning. He seemed to regard a book as something sacred, and nothing more quickly stirred his youthful indignation than the mutilation of one of his idols. After he had learned to read, such was his unremitting devotion to his studies that his father was often obliged to hide his books away from him. His ability gave him an easy pre-eminence in scholarship. In the district school which he attended, no boy equaled his readiness in mastering his lessons, or his fearlessness in venturing upon dangerous enterprises. His intrepidity amounted to temerity. But his perilous adventures were never prompted by a spirit of wild and vicious daring. His nature was rich and exuberant, full of buoyant and elastic life. His enthusiasm, bravery, and kindness toward all made him a natural leader. His little mates loved to acknowledge his supremacy. In school, he was obedient and studious; out of doors, he was full of all kinds of innocent frolic and daring. The first scholar was also the best wrestler. Throughout life he retained his early fondness for active sports. The dignified chancellor, like the Roman senator, thought it not beneath his position to participate in the pastimes of youth. Though impulsive and capable of anger, he was full of exuberant and irrepressible good nature. Even in his sports, he was careful not to wound the feelings of his playmates. He often walked to church with poor boys to avoid any appearance of superiority. He used to commit to memory long passages of Scripture for the Sabbath school, but was unwilling to recite all he had learned for fear of mortifying the feelings of his young classmates.

In early youth, his opportunities for obtaining an education were limited. Till he was sixteen, he was able to attend the public school only three months out of the year; the rest of the time he worked on his father's farm. In his seventeenth year, he attended the academy at Hopkinton, New Hampshire, and taught school the following winter in Concord, New Hampshire. This was the commencement of his remarkable career as a teacher. In his eighteenth year, he bade a final adieu to the farm, and entered the Teachers' Seminary, Andover, Massachusetts, to study mathematics. The succeeding winter he was engaged, at the suggestion of Samuel R. Hall, the

Principal of the Teachers' Seminary, to teach school at West Newbury.

The circumstances which attended this selection were highly creditable to Mr. Hoyt. The school was large and difficult to manage. The pupils took a vicious pride in resisting the authority of the instructor. They had ejected several teachers from the school-house with rude violence. But Mr. Hoyt soon taught the insurgents a lesson of loyal obedience to the constituted authorities. Under his discipline the school was eminently successful.

At this period of his life, the Rev. J. Q. A. Egell, impressed with his display of talents, urged him to go to college. Persuaded by his friendly arguments, Mr. Hoyt returned to the academy at Hopkinton, and went through the preparatory course. He afterward reviewed his academic studies at Andover.

The officers of the Normal School, and of the Hopkinton and Andover Academies, soon detected Mr. Hoyt's varied and extraordinary capacities for instruction, and employed him as an assistant teacher. During his preparatory pupilage he was both student and instructor in these three institutions. At Andover, during the temporary absence of Professor Barton—who was employed by the Government in the survey of the Northeastern Boundary—the youthful student took charge of three classes in mathematics. For four months Mr. Hoyt discharged the duties of professor, and at the same time kept up his own studies. In the twofold and thrice sustained relation of pupil and teacher, neither the arduous duties of instruction prevented him from attaining the foremost rank in his class, nor did the familiarity with which scholars are wont to regard a fellow-student defeat his prosperity as teacher.

Before going to college, Mr. Hoyt taught school five winters, exclusive of his academic tuition. In all of these schools he exhibited those higher qualities of the successful teacher for which he was so distinguished in later life.

In 1836 he entered Yale College without conditions. Notwithstanding the difficulties which had beset his academic course, his preparation was thorough. He was distinguished at Yale for superior scholarship, forensic ability, originality of thought and expression, the strength of his friendships, and his magnetic power over his associates. During his collegiate course he took prizes for excellence in mathematical studies and in English composition. He was graduated with high honors. His part at Commencement was an oration. He was sixth scholar in a class of one hundred. Of his high scholarship, Jeremiah Day, who was President of Yale while Mr. Hoyt was a member of that institution, bears the following honorable testimony: "Mr. Hoyt," writes the venerable ex-president, "was a distinguished scholar, being appointed an orator for the Commencement day when he was graduated. I do not recollect for what department of literature and science he was particularly partial, for he made himself master of all. He was earnestly devoted to thorough investigation."

While in college, he was chosen one of the editors of the *Yale Literary Magazine*, and was elected, by an almost unanimous vote, President of the Brothers in

Unity. His articles in the magazine, and his decisions as president of the society, bore marks of unusual ability and sound judgment.

His classmates describe Mr. Hoyt as being very fond, in his college days, of social pleasures, keen in good-natured raillery and repartee, and overflowing with a wit whose comic and original combinations set the college table in a roar.

In the spring of 1840, Mr. Hoyt took charge of an academy at Plymouth, New Hampshire. His acceptance of this trust placed him at the head of a school of two hundred scholars. But he was fully equal to the responsibilities of his position. His popularity in the management of this large institution was based upon true success.

In 1841 Mr. Hoyt was appointed Professor of Mathematics and Natural Philosophy in Phillips' Academy, Exeter, New Hampshire. He remained in this institution eighteen years. It was the scene of his life-labors. From its classic halls a generation of students went forth into the world, disciplined by his generous culture.

Phillips' Exeter Academy is one of the very best preparatory institutions in the land, and much of its excellence is due to the improvements which Professor Hoyt introduced.

April 13th, 1842, Mr. Hoyt married Margarette T. Chamberlain, of Exeter. The issue of this marriage was a family of six children, five of whom—three sons and two daughters—survive their father.

In 1845 Mr. Hoyt revised Colton's Greek Reader, and added a new vocabulary of his own preparation. This lexicon is a work of superior excellence. It was composed with a careful and scholarly attention to etymologies, the primary and secondary meanings of words, and the order of their derivation.

In 1851 Mr. Hoyt was a member of the Convention for the revision of the State Constitution, and took an important part in the deliberations of that body.

In 1858 he barely escaped a Congressional nomination. Had he remained in New Hampshire, he would undoubtedly have been honored with the highest civic trusts in the gift of the State.

In December, 1858, he accepted the appointment of Chancellor and Professor of the Greek Language and Literature in Washington University, St. Louis. He entered upon the duties of his new position the following February, and was formally inaugurated October 4th, 1859.

In July, 1859, he received from Dartmouth College the degree of Doctor of Laws.

In the fall of 1860 Chancellor Hoyt's health began to fail, and alarming symptoms of consumption began to develop themselves. Impelled by anxiety to regain his health, he tested the virtues of various medicines and systems of treatment, breathed the pure and bracing airs of Minnesota, and tried the dry and equable climate at the head waters of the Missouri. But all his efforts were ineffectual. With many illusions of improvement and recovery, he gradually sank, and, after a protracted illness of constant and increasing suffering, expired at his residence in St. Louis, November 26th, 1862.

In physical characteristics, Chancellor Hoyt was of medium height and manly figure. His complexion was light, and his face, during all the years of man-

hood, wore the scholar's livery of thoughtful paleness.
But though pallid, he was very strong. Few men
possessed equal power of muscle. His head was
large and well rounded, his brow high and ample,
and his features sharply defined, and indicative of
keen perceptions and of great force and marked indi-
viduality of character. He was fortunate in the accidents of physical constitution. His strong and
well-balanced mind was united with a sanguine and
sensitive temperament. In his happy organization
were found the conditions most favorable to intellectual greatness. His countenance was frank and
open, and expressions of honesty were written in
plain and legible characters all over his manly features. Shortly after he came to St. Louis, and while
he was yet a stranger in our midst, he found himself
one day at the post-office without any change to pay
his postage. A less direct and original man would
have waited till another occasion. But Chancellor
Hoyt, as soon as he discovered his poverty, walked to
a neighboring stand, took off his hat, and asked the
newsboy if he looked like an honest man. "Yes,
sir," was the quick and emphatic reply. "Then
lend me a quarter." The honest face was a sufficient
guarantee of payment; the boy trusted him, and was
not the victim of misplaced confidence.

The presence of Chancellor Hoyt was kindly and
prepossessing. The attraction of his genial bearing
extended far beyond the circle of his immediate
friends, and drew to himself, with magnetic gravita-
tion, large numbers of strangers.

As a citizen of Exeter, Mr. Hoyt was foremost in

every enterprise of public moment. Every measure for the improvement of the town, for the advancement of education, for the promotion of public interests, received his efficient support. The beautiful school-houses, the public institutions, and improved appearance of that quiet village are largely due to his personal efforts. Mr. Hoyt's services in behalf of popular education were unremitting and signally beneficial. With his own hand he drafted the plan of a model school-house, and elaborated all the parts with such niceness of detail as to determine, with philosophical care, the angle of seat and desk best adapted to ease and health.

His plan was widely adopted in the southeastern portion of the State, and proved a blessing to many youth. A thorough ventilation prevented the headaches and weariness caused by the respiration of poisoned air, while the arrangement of seats and the adaptation of rooms greatly facilitated the labors of teachers. But Mr. Hoyt was not alone in his endeavors to introduce school-houses of improved architecture. The merit of this success is equally to be attributed to the practical suggestions and able co-operation of Judge French.

Of Mr. Hoyt's practical skill in drafting, the school-houses at the East are not the only monuments. The design of erecting an observatory, and adding to the University buildings a new front on Washington Avenue, originated with Mr. Hoyt; and he even sketched the details of construction. The building which he projected not only contained all the accommodations of the present structure, but was adorned with a very beautiful and imposing façade. But the funds of the University did not justify the adoption of the plan which good taste had conceived.

Mr. Hoyt strove to add to tasteful architecture the charms of fine scenery, that the influences of beauty might elevate the minds of the pupils, and that the memories of manhood might linger in delighted association around the scene of early instruction. Professor Hoyt's efforts raised the standard of scholarship throughout the public schools of the State. He was many years superintendent of the common schools of Exeter. During his tenure of this trust, he never allowed his kindliness of nature to interfere with his sense of duty. He never retained an incompetent teacher through infirmity of will or indisposition to give offense. He introduced into the public schools of Exeter an improved classification, better systems of teaching, more efficient instructors, and roused pupils and teachers to new activity by his own fervid enthusiasm. He reduced all the different schools to three classes—the primary, grammar, and high school—and prescribed the course of study which is now pursued in the several grades.

His school reports were written with a brilliancy and wisdom seldom equalled in that kind of literature. One of these, in particular, was so full of wit, originality, and sound suggestion, that the entire report was, in some instances, copied by the press, and extracts found their way into nearly every paper in the land.

The High School building—one of the chief ornaments of Exeter—is another enduring proof of Professor Hoyt's interest in popular education. The erection of this beautiful and well-planned structure was due to his personal efforts.

The usefulness of town libraries did not escape the observation of a mind keenly alive to every means of social improvement. Professor Hoyt was active in the establishment of a public library at Exeter, and helped by material aid to fill its alcoves with sound literature, and to afford to every inhabitant of the village ampler opportunities of cultivated enjoyment. Remote generations of Exeter youth will bless the memory of him who placed within their reach the advantages of sound culture.

In watching the practical effects of the existing system of education, Mr. Hoyt soon observed that teachers, remote from each other and from the incitements of honorable competition, and often invited to negligence by a lax and incompetent supervision, are apt to lose their interest in their professional duties, and fall into habits of mere routine. Thinking that frequent conventions of teachers would counteract this downward tendency, Mr. Hoyt was among the first to recommend the adoption of teachers' institutes. The success of the plan realized his expectations. The institutes tended to test competency, to exact higher qualifications, to revive enthusiasm, to impart new systems of instruction and better solutions of difficulties, and to subject teachers to more intelligent and rigorous surveillance. The influence of this normal instruction and comparison of methods was measurably felt in all the public schools of the Commonwealth.

During Mr. Hoyt's residence at Exeter, he strenuously advocated the erection of a town hall. In this,
and every other generous rivalry of public spirit,
Hon. Amos Tuck and Judge H. F. French were his
competitors. The combined efforts of this friendly
triumvirate were successful, and now a beautiful and
spacious edifice, adapted to the political and social
wants of the community, adorns the village.

He introduced into the Exeter Lyceum, of which
he was one of the ablest members, a device to test
native talent and develop powers of extemporaneous
speech. After the meeting of the Lyceum, a committee was appointed to select the subject of debate for
that evening. The disputants were chosen by lot,
and were subject to a fine if they did not speak five
minutes on the question before the Society. To
guard against all possible collusion, the members of
the committee were not allowed to participate in the
discussion. This arrangement, affording no opportunity for preparation, and throwing the debaters
upon their own resources, was not only productive of
personal improvement, but of infinite entertainment.

Professor Hoyt's public spirit was again manifest in
his efforts to beautify Exeter. He loved trees. He
felt almost a personal affection for them. He remarked of himself, that "his knowledge of trees was
second only to his acquaintance with Greek and
mathematics." The best varieties of fruit and shade
trees ornamented his grounds; and in the summer
season he was wont to cultivate them with daily
labor, and with scientific care to protect their growth
from the inroads of insects. One of his ablest essays

is on this favorite subject. Fifteen years ago he urged the citizens of Exeter to adorn the town with trees, and now the villagers walk streets embowered in emerald beauty and cool with sylvan shade. His mortal remains now repose in dreamless slumber under the tree which years ago his own hand planted. Exeter owes a debt of lasting gratitude to the scholarly citizen whose public spirit and liberal enterprise have contributed so much to its improvement.

One of the first traits that attracts attention in an analysis of Chancellor Hoyt's character is his physical and moral courage. His nature abounded in a plentiful lack of cowardice. An incapacity of fear and great presence of mind in danger carried him safe through many scenes of peril.

When Mr. Hoyt was at Dunbarton, a party of scholars went out one day on a bathing excursion, and one of the number, while engaged in the sport of diving, became entangled in some sunken brushwood, and was in danger of drowning. The other scholars were frightened and irresolute, but Mr. Hoyt, thoughtless of personal exposure, instantly swam to the rescue, and, plunging, extricated the drowning youth from his entanglement, and tried to swim ashore with him; but the helpless and unconscious burden weighed him down beneath the waters. Still he did not relax his hold, but sinking with his friend dragged him along the bottom of the pond. Twice he was obliged to come to the surface to take breath, and twice he returned to the rescue. At last, almost exhausted by his exertions, he brought his schoolmate safe to land, and enjoyed the satisfaction of having saved his life.

When Mr. Hoyt was in college, he was grossly insulted by a student of large and athletic frame. The bully was disposed to take unfair advantage of his physical superiority; but he suddenly found himself

> " Laid low,
> With his back to the field and his feet to the foe,"

and learned, by personal chastisement, the danger of insulting a brave man. From this time Mr. Hoyt was the acknowledged champion of his class, and no one ever afterward ventured to test his powers of self-defense.

Once when Mr. Hoyt was traveling on the Boston and Albany road, his journey was interrupted at Springfield by the reparation of the bridge which spans the Connecticut at that point. Mr. Hoyt, impatient to take the train which stood in readiness on the opposite bank, did not wait for the slow ferry, but attempted, though encumbered with a heavy carpet-sack, to cross over the remnants of the bridge. His pathway was long and dangerous. Sometimes only narrow and unfastened timbers, or a single, unsteady plank, lay between him and the broad waters of the Connecticut. It was a feat calculated to test the strongest nerves. Hundreds of spectators watched his progress with anxious interest. But his steadiness and self-possession carried him safe across.

Mr. Hoyt's moral bravery was fearless of persons or consequences. In his loyalty to truth he was unmoved by popular prejudices or the fashionable opinions of the hour. The wreck of worlds could not shake him from his convictions. His independence almost exceeded the limits of prudence. In the performance of duty he was utterly careless of human opposition. He had no reverence for mere station. Politicians without statesmanship, aristocrats without worth, *savans* without learning, patriots without loyalty, were objects of his unqualified contempt. The penniless child of want, enriched with wealth of heart and head, stood far higher in his esteem than a profligate and senseless millionaire. His erect manhood could never prosper by the thrift that follows fawning. In his eyes adversity did not dishonor virtue, nor success dignify vice. With him popularity was no test of truth, nor were the idols of the hour the objects of his worship. Independent, fearless, and true to his own nature, neither the solicitations of interest nor the pressure of local opinions could ever induce him to desert the convictions of enlightened reason.

I have never known an instance of more invincible will. The powers of sickness could not conquer his energy of mind. His intellect seemed clear to the last moment of life. He attended to his professional duties when he was too weak to ascend the steps of the University without assistance. He revised his essays for the press when prostrate upon the fatal couch and unable even to sit up in bed. His hold upon life was strong. The near prospect of death at times moved him to tears. But it was no mere attachment to sensuous life that occasioned his regrets. In many conversations he expressed a strong desire to live, not for the pleasures of sense or the conscious joy of existence, but because he thought he could be of service to his family and to society. He deplored the sad fate which arrested the course of life in mid career, and frustrated all his purposes of public usefulness. His determination to live for the sake of doing good was the secret of his wonderful tenacity of life. In a human and physiological sense, his unconquerable will repulsed death and added months to his term of life.

Akin to this spirit of moral intrepidity were his qualities of brave and tireless energy. Defeats did not discourage him. If obstacles obstructed his pathway they only strengthened his resolution to surmount them. He was determined to conquer success. A nature thus assured of ultimate triumph is already half victorious.

His father's unwillingness to defray the expenses of his education threw him upon his own resources. At Andover he earned, by manual toil, the means of continuing his studies. In order to appreciate fully the degree of perseverance which this fact discloses, it is necessary to remember that he not only maintained his position in the front rank of his class, but was also at the same time an assistant teacher in the Academy. He was thus performing, with an unusual measure of success, the threefold duties of student, instructor, and manual laborer.

At Yale he was again dependent, to a great extent, upon his own efforts for the means of prosecuting his studies. Moved by pecuniary considerations, he resorted to the novel economy of abridging his college

course. The Faculty granted him permission to omit
the intermediate year and enter the Junior Class, on
the condition that he passed a satisfactory examination in the studies of the Sophomore year. A mastery of the studies pursued at Yale demands the best
talents and industry of the students. But the brilliant young Freshman assumed a double task, and
performed the labors of the twofold course with eminent success. The difficulties of the undertaking
were increased by the fact that the Sophomore course
presupposed a knowledge of Freshman studies, which
he had not yet been over. Yet he fully maintained
his standing in his own class, and prosecuted success-
fully the studies of the Sophomore year till his eyes,
impaired by excessive application, defeated his hopes
in the moment of victory. In the gloom of a dark-
ened chamber he had ample opportunity to regret the
overtasking of his physical powers. His inflamed
eyes were nature's protest against his studious impru-
dence. Had it not been for this unfortunate failure
of eyesight, he would certainly have accomplished his
purpose.

His professional career at Exeter furnishes many
illustrations of his persistency of character. Phillips'
Academy, at the time Mr. Hoyt became connected
with it, lacked rigid classification. He proposed to
reduce all the classes to four. But it was thought
impolitic to disturb, with any untried innovations, a
system that had, with fair success, withstood the test
of experience. It was alleged that students of different capacities and various attainments could not
be advantageously subjected to so rigorous a classifi-

cation. But the great success which crowned the final adoption of Professor Hoyt's plan showed its wisdom. Perhaps no one measure in the history of the institution conduced more to the elevation and excellence of the Academy.

Prior to Mr. Hoyt's connection with Phillips' Academy, the students were required to study in the building. The fatal objections to this system did not long escape Mr. Hoyt's sagacity. The students were too mature to be treated like little boys. Subject to all the interruptions and distractions of a class-room in which recitations were conducted, the pupils necessarily lost much time. Study under the eye of a teacher, Mr. Hoyt asserted, was unfavorable to personal independence and undirected research; yet it was an essential duty of educators to cultivate habits of self-control and original investigation. It was the policy of the institution to dismiss from its halls all those students in whom a generous confidence could not be reposed. The Academy was instituted for the benefit of high-minded youth earnestly engaged in the work of self-culture. This temple, sacred to polite learning, should bear upon its front, in a literature of gold, the inspired command of the Sibyl, "Procul, profani." Its shrines should not be polluted by undevout and impure devotees; merit and capacity should be the tests of admission; honorable deportment and successful scholarship the conditions of membership. Good order and manly conduct should not be so much the result of coercive authority as of moral principle and a high-toned sense of propriety. These considerations ultimately prevailed, and the change was highly beneficial to the Academy.

When Mr. Hoyt first went to Exeter, he observed that the high price of board in that village was a serious injury to the Academy. Education in those halls was too costly a luxury for students of moderate means. The consequence was that the members of the Academy were mostly from two widely divergent conditions in life. The sons of the wealthy were sent for the sake of nominal distinction, while indigent students came to secure the cheap culture which the charity foundations furnished; but the middle class, possessing a mere competency, and independently paying their own way, could not afford this expensive education. To remedy this defect, Professor Hoyt strongly urged the erection of a commons hall. This plan did not originate with him, but its successful execution was greatly facilitated by his earnest exertions. A building, named Abbot Hall, was erected, with accommodations for fifty students. The new arrangement reduced the price of board one-half, and at once brought into the Academy a new class of students. Prior to this, the influence of the rich members, who are not generally the most studious and exemplary pupils, withheld the Academy from its highest excellence. But the honorable and aspiring youth who now entered its halls set an example of manly bearing and earnest study, which controlled the public sentiment of the school, stimulated wealthy idlers to greater industry, shamed the vicious into better habits, and contributed largely to the fame and usefulness of the institution.

But most of these reforms were strenuously opposed. Year after year the measures which have since proved

so beneficial were voted down. Yet Professor Hoyt
renewed his efforts till ultimate success rewarded his
perseverance. Only an energy ignorant of defeat,
and persistent under the discouragements of repeated
failure, could have achieved these victories. I do not
wish to convey the impression that Mr. Hoyt originated all of these reforms, or that he was the sole cause
of their introduction. He had able coadjutors in Dr.
Soule, Hon. Amos Tuck, Dr. Peabody, and other
members of the Faculty and Board of Trust. But
the representations which have reached me since Mr.
Hoyt's death—upon which my own statements are
based—leave no doubt that he was the most active,
untiring, and efficient advocate of those measures
which have raised Phillips' Exeter Academy almost
to the level of our colleges.

Chancellor Hoyt was master of all the higher arts
and noble secrets of discipline. The remark which
he made of Dr. Abbot is eminently true of himself—
no one better understood the nature of young men.
With native skill he swept the lyre of the human
heart and held its chords in easy mastery. He sympathized deeply with his students. His own experience was too fresh in his mind for him to forget the
trials and temptations, the labors and joys of student
life. He made no pretensions to learning he did not
possess. If he made a mistake, he frankly confessed
it. Such intellectual candor always commands the
admiration of ingenuous youth. No motives of personal partiality ever led him from strict justice in his
treatment of students. Neither wealth nor social
position ever shielded an offender from deserved

punishment. He was animated by a strong and unaffected desire to benefit and befriend students. Their personal welfare was always the object of his friendly solicitude. His keen wit enlivened the sobriety of the class-room, and his happy faculty of illustration elucidated every obscurity. His fresh and varied scholarship, instinct with learned enthusiasm and vital with practical applications, inspired his students with a new and deeper devotion to learning, and a generous emulation of his example. His rich and rigorous instruction reared, firm and enduring, the architecture of an elegant and ample scholarship. Thus he controlled students by the influence of a manly character, and by the fine magnetism of a noble and gifted nature. Under his tuition, pupils became too manly for mean pranks, or forgot their disposition to mischief in their devotion to study. He stimulated scholars to studious toil by no system of rewards and punishments, but impressed upon them the priceless value of culture and the duty of self-development. His students, though subjected to strict discipline, were almost unconscious of control, and their sense of personal independence was not offended by a rude exercise of authority. Yet Mr. Hoyt, with all his native kindliness, was capable of strong indignation. In his intercourse with youth, he always appealed to their nobler instincts, and reposed trust in their sense of honor. Grief, speedy and poignant, overtook any betrayal of that confidence. Frank himself, he hated deceit in others. Whenever any unmanly act provoked his censure, he was wont to give the offender what he quaintly called "a specimen of extemporaneous eloquence," and it was a kind of rhetoric strikingly calculated to touch the feelings and linger in the memory of the hearer. The student was very apt to be content with one specimen of this oratory.

Chancellor Hoyt greatly admired Dr. Arnold, and unostentatiously emulated his career. His profession led him to reflect deeply upon the problems of education, and his own system of instruction indicated his solution. Like the great teacher of Rugby, he thought any system of education radically defective which did not make true manliness the prime object of culture. He believed that vice became more dangerous by cultivation, that scholarship should only grace manly virtues, that nobility of character should be the primary condition of admission to literary institutions, that only pure worshipers were entitled to enter the temple of learning. In intellectual discipline, he considered it of far higher importance to teach the mind habits of accurate thought than to crowd the memory with facts. Beyond any teacher I have ever known —with perhaps a single exception—he had the faculty to kindle enthusiasm in students, to reconcile them, by the attractions of his instruction, to the toils of scholarship, to develop powers of reasoning, to quicken the present sense of duty by truths twenty centuries old, and to show that the thoughts of the dead past are yet instinct with life and wisdom, and applicable still to the conditions of human society.

Chancellor Hoyt had great powers of acquisition. He was capable of close and protracted application. His mind possessed an intuitive quickness of apprehension. A distinguished judge mentions his fondness for law cases, and the professional acumen with which he at once comprehended difficult technical points. Mr. Hoyt possessed those high natural qualities and adaptations of mind which especially fitted him to succeed in the walks of law or statesmanship. His investigations were rapid and exhaustive. At the time he thought of going to Cuba to try the virtues of a tropic climate, he learned the Spanish language in *one month*, so that he read it with the same facility that he did Latin. With the true instinct of genius, he always perceived the essential points of a subject, and marshaled his facts about them.

His learning became a part of his intellectual being, and circulated in the currents of mental life. All his knowledge was ready for instant use. His various scholarship was kept organized and disciplined for immediate action. He perceived the subtile relationship of apparently unconnected truths, and summoned remote facts to the common defense of right or overthrow of wrong.

Chancellor Hoyt's scholarship was rich and accurate. His special devotion to Greek arose from the accidents of his position .at Exeter; the natural sciences were his favorite studies. He was a natural mathematician. His inborn aptitude for mathematical studies showed itself everywhere. At school and in college, his intuitive perception of mathematical truths and relations gave him an easy eminence in the science of calculation. He once told me that he never tried a problem that he did not solve, but immediately added, with a humor that never deserted

him, that he was careful not to try the hardest ones.
An extravagant statement was quickly reduced to the
dimensions of truth by the merciless logic of figures.
He tried everything by the stern test of numbers. If
you should meet him upon the street on a cold winter's day, and ask him how many shingles it would
take to cover a roof of irregular shape and varying
angles, he would forget external cold in the ardor of
calculation. Nor would he keep you long in shiver-
ing expectation of an answer. Proficients in figures,
with the advantage of pencil and paper, often found
themselves perplexed by problems which he solved
by quick processes of mental arithmetic. Teachers,
lawyers, and judges sought the aid of his mathematical ability. On one occasion Professor Hoyt recom-
mended to the citizens of Exeter the erection of a
large and expensive school-house. A public meeting
was called, and the plan was violently opposed. The
opponents of the measure dwelt upon the magnitude
of the sum to be raised, and the heavy burden the
assessment would impose upon the poor tax-payers.
At last, when the project seemed certain to fail, Professor Hoyt rose, and quietly stated the valuation of
the town, the amount of taxable property, the number of ratable polls, and the cost of the proposed building; then, going to the board, he "ciphered out," in
the presence of the voters, the exact sum which each
poll would have to pay. And when it was shown, by
mathematical demonstration, that the humblest citizen
would have to contribute only twenty-five cents, in
order to enjoy the privilege of educating his children
in a more healthful and elegant school-house, the
measure was carried almost by acclamation.

His memory of figures was truly wonderful. He rarely dealt in round numbers, because it was equally easy to cite the precise figures. When he was a member of the Convention, he often surprised that body by the extent and accuracy of his statistical information. In college, Mr. Hoyt aspired to the highest mathematical honors of his class. There was but one student who could endanger his supremacy; and the growing reputation of his rival must have touched his sensitive ambition. But his bosom was not the residence of mean jealousies; and, instead of cherishing secret feelings of envy, Mr. Hoyt went to the room of his competitor, and asked to see his solutions. Struck with the proofs of superior mathematical genius and with the scientific precision and simplicity of his demonstrations, the ingenuous Freshman, with a nobility of soul that mingles love with our admiration, at once acknowledged the pre-eminence of his rival. His defeated hopes found solace in generous and appreciative recognition of excellence. This pleasant incident, so honorable to both parties, strengthened a slight and casual acquaintance into a warm and life-long attachment. To this magnanimity and friendship Washington University owes one of its brightest ornaments.

Chancellor Hoyt was a growing and progressive man. His interest in life expired only with his breath. His aggressive and acquisitive studies were constantly adding new fields to his intellectual estate, and opening broader views over the landscapes of knowledge. His mind never lost its early elasticity and power of acquisition. He kept up with the progress of positive science and of speculative philosophy.

His power of strong and wholesome assimilation incorporated every nutritive fact into the very structure of his mind, and strengthened every faculty into vigorous and healthful activity. He was never afflicted with symptoms of ossification — no cabinet of fossils could claim him. He was a thoroughly live man, vital in every part, warm with glowing interest in every enterprise for the improvement of mankind, and quickened with active sympathy for every form of human misery.

The most conspicuous intellectual trait of Chancellor Hoyt was sound sense. An exclusive devotion to learning is apt to unfit men for business and practical judgment; but the Chancellor did not lose the homely virtue of common sense in the retired pursuits of polite study. What first arrests attention in his writings is not the sinewy vigor of his style, but the solid wisdom of his thoughts; and, in his social intercourse, he appeared to be less a scholar than a sagacious and thoughtful man of the world. His ideas on general subjects were liberal and catholic. He never narrowed his mind to mere selfish or partial views. Conservative of whatever has the sanctions of time, he yet belonged, by constitution and temperament, to the progressive school of thinkers. Impelled by his impatience of present evils, he zealously advocated every judicious reform.

Chancellor Hoyt was a man of brilliant wit. This power, dangerous in the hands of those who love the flash and the stroke, careless of the wounds they inflict, was only used by him to grace the gentle offices of friendship or promote the ends of truth. No mere wanton love of display ever led him to pain the sensibilities of his friends. From their bosoms, his wit

"Ne'er bore a heart-stain away on its blade;"

but it fell keen and trenchant upon all the enemies of virtue. The wit which shed a genial glow over all the innocent pursuits of life, hurled its scathing lightnings full on the head of all dishonor and injustice. His wit usually contained an argument. In the old Swampscot House at Exeter, the drinking saloon occupied the most prominent and accessible room on the ground-floor. After this building was burned, a new hotel was erected on the same site, in which the bar-room was placed in the basement. Mr. Hoyt said the change was a wise one, but that the bar-room should have been sunk fifty feet lower, on the architectural principle that the porch, and the edifice into which it leads, should be as near together as possible. Of the wit which produced explosive laughter, the sobriety of this occasion will not permit me to give illustrations.

Chancellor Hoyt excelled in powers of ready argument and lucid statement. His mind was as clear as a diamond; and it had,

"With the flash of the gem, its solidity too."

His skill in maintaining a theory was remarkable. Sometimes, in social sport and mere wantonness of logic, he would defend some wretched fallacy; but, under his treatment, the outcast became respectable, and assumed the garb of reason. In public discussion, his strength of argument, facility of expression, original wit, and ready improvement of passing incidents, rendered him a powerful and popular speaker. It is no friendly exaggeration of his forensic abilities to say that he never made a speech that was not a signal success. I have often heard him on festal and serious occasions, but never without fresh admiration of his "incisive logic," his clear and comprehensive views, his novel combinations of familiar facts, and his creative energy of thought and diction. At Yale, he was among the foremost debaters in college. It is a custom at Yale for each Society to elect an orator, to present its claims before the Freshmen. Mr. Hoyt was chosen to speak in behalf of the Brothers in Unity. The point, felicity, and fervor of his address made an impression on the minds of his fellow-students, which the lapse of twenty Lethean years has not effaced. In extemporaneous debate, he had a remarkable faculty of exciting interest in his subject, and of breathing a warm and generous life into the inanimate learning of bygone ages. He could command at will the resources of ridicule and sarcasm, of argument and impassioned declamation.

The main characteristics of Chancellor Hoyt's style are clearness and energy. The current of thought is full, clear, and rapid. Vigor was the happy necessity of his intellectual organization. His mind found natural utterance in no other form of expression. His writings are full of the trophies of intellectual conquest. They are crowded, too, with quick and affectionate recognitions of the beautiful in nature and the poetic in art.

Chancellor Hoyt never wore a mask nor trod the tragic buskin. He said common things in a simple way. His style was adapted to his subject, and rose with the grandeur of the theme. Sometimes, however, his hate of pedantry and love of point led him to borrow, from the speech of daily life, homely illustrations, and expressions more remarkable for vigor than elegance. But good taste was not often sacrificed to energy. Mr. Hoyt wrote on a great variety of subjects. Politics, education, music, agriculture, criticism, tile-draining, potatoes, and insects are some of the topics that engaged his fruitful pen. He was a frequent contributor to the pages of the *North American Review*. During the last ten years of his residence at the East he delivered public lectures. Notwithstanding the confinement of his professional duties, he sometimes lectured twenty-five times in the course of a single winter. Normal Schools and Teachers' Institutes often engaged the service of his vigorous pen.

Mr. Hoyt was fond of showing his productions to his friends, for the sake of their criticism; and a good suggestion, though it emanated from the humblest source, was always adopted. He discussed whatever subject he touched with strong sense, and enriched it with a wealth gathered in the mines of learning. He was a mineralogist in the placers of knowledge. He knew where the auriferous deposits lay. His scholarship grew rich by prosperous mining and original speculation. Some classic allusion, some apposite quotation, some unexpected application of philosophy showed that a man of culture and sense was treating the theme.

Chancellor Hoyt was a man of poetic sensibilities. In his writings, we occasionally meet passages fragrant with the bloom and flowerage of poetry. His illustrations are often ornate with images of rich and original beauty. His imagination wandered amid loveliness of its own creation. His word-pictures sometimes have a Titian depth of coloring. He had an æsthetic taste. His eye lingered with delight upon the gentle beauty of the flower, the pomp of sunset glory, the wild grandeur of mountain scenery. The voices of nature, unheard by common ears, spoke to him with Naiad eloquence. He loved the sweet harmonies of music. He had listened with a sense of exquisite satisfaction to the matin orisons of birds; the sweet undertones in which enamored winds whisper to the trees; "the quiet evening tune of the waterfall, not heard by day; and the voices, now hushed, which once sang around the ample, ever-blazing hearthstone." What a sweet and tender appreciation of nature breathes through the following passage:—

"Shakspeare has said there are 'tongues in trees.' To the truth of this assertion of the great poet we yield our willing testimony, for we have often heard them speak ourselves. Their tongues are the expanding bud of spring and the sere and yellow leaf of autumn. Their teachings are for all. Their sound has gone into all the earth. The lone pine, which kindly overshadowed our youthful pastimes, was wont at the sunset hour to whisper to us, as with a spirit's voice, and tell us strange tales, which we shall not soon forget. In the far-reaching aisles of our sunless forests, too, we have often listened to the deep and varied tones, till we have ceased to wonder that the sacred oaks of Dodona were living, speaking oracles to the simple-minded, nature-loving Greeks. But nature speaks not merely in the tree. She has a thousand voices. She may be heard in the harsh tones of the live thunder, and in the nameless yet delicious harmonies of a summer's evening; in the sepulchral moanings of the night-wind that wails around our window, and in the morning melody of merry birds; in the tireless tossings of the dark-blue ocean, and in the cheerful murmurings of the loquacious brook; in the lowing herds on the hill-side, and in the song which comes, like angel music, from some happy heart."

Mr. Hoyt's mind was richly stored with the treasures of poetry. Indeed he sometimes wrote poetry himself. The following lines, from verses which Mr. Hoyt wrote on the death of a young lady, breathe the hopes of an immortal faith, and stir meditations within us which console our present grief.

"This life is but a vapor wreath,
Illumed with morning's golden light;
A silver stream, whose cooling flow
The bending reed and flower laves;
A fragile harp, whose tuneful strings
Are gently swept by zephyr's breath;
So frail a thing is human life;
How slight a boon for God to give,
If, with the dying spirit's frame,
Thought and affection cease to live.

"But no! the harp, new-tuned above,
Shall bend in music with the throng
Whose lofty anthems ever rise
Amid a glorious world of song.
O! think not that the life is lost,
Which wanders from your sight afar;
The star, though hid behind the cloud,
Is still a bright and shining star."

Mr. Hoyt had made the great master of English tragedy the subject of profound study. Though reared on a farm, with few early opportunities of elegant culture, yet when in college he seemed to know Shakspeare by heart. Every incident of daily life, whether of a grave or festive character, brought an apt quotation to his lips. It was the custom of the presidents elect of the Brothers in Unity to deliver to the Society an elaborate address. But Mr. Hoyt, instead of following the precedent, simply said, "Brothers, you have taken me by surprise. I have no speech ready. I can only tell you that

'I am no orator—
But, as you know me all, a plain, blunt man,
That love my friend; and that they know full well
That gave me public leave to speak'—

I will do the best I can to serve you." The members showed their appreciation of the pertinent and happy quotation by expressions of hearty applause.

The influence of his poetic studies is visible in Chancellor Hoyt's writings. No man can touch Shakspeare without improvement. By this antean contact of mind the faculties are strengthened. What the Chancellor said of the study of the classics is equally true of the study of Shakspeare. "We cannot wander through Sabean groves of bloom without catching the perfume in our dress; we cannot 'sit down to a symposium with the gods and rise from the banquet wholly mortal.'" Communion with Shakspeare's master mind imparted to Mr. Hoyt's style a grace and Saxon purity of expression. He caught from this ennobling intimacy elegance and dignity of intellectual bearing.

But logic was the imperial faculty of his mind; and the sovereign, jealous of rivals, often suppressed the rising imagination. The ascendency of the reasoning powers was unfavorable to the development of creative fancy.

There was in Chancellor Hoyt a rare combination of abstruse science and poetic imagination. These qualities, so opposite and so seldom united, gave richness and varied charms to his intellectual character. His mental pathway did not wind, with intentional deviations, among flowery meads, till the traveler, fatigued with beauty, became weary of the way. But the road led with logical directness to its destination; and the flowerets by the wayside delighted, while they did not delay, the journey. His thought was never crushed with Tarpeian accumulations of ornament; the glitter of spear and buckler only made his sturdy logic more formidable.

It was fortunate for the University that Chancellor Hoyt was endowed with such various gifts. It is seldom that a scholar is distinguished in more than one department of study. His talent for mathematics was his highest gift; but yet he was one of the best practical teachers of Greek I have ever known.

There are doubtless men in the country more learned in Hellenic lore, but I have never met a scholar who united in a higher degree rich Greek learning with remarkable capacity for instruction. This combination of science and literature is of the highest value to the head of a university. His various scholarship enabled the Chancellor to determine for himself the proportionate importance which each department ought to assume in a symmetrical system of study. Nor was the Chancellor obliged to rely upon the fidelity and supposed competency of his brother officers; his own knowledge was adequate to decide upon their qualifications and the measure of their success. His native judgment, strengthened by long experience in practical instruction, and his wide range of study peculiarly fitted him to co-ordinate departments into their due relations, and to mature a system of university education adapted to the conditions of Western life; and his high administrative abilities enabled him to carry into successful execution the plans which his sagacity had originated.

Chancellor Hoyt devoted much time and reflection to affairs of public moment. The Federalist was one of his favorite books. Few statesmen in the land were more deeply read in the works of Hamilton, Madison, and Jefferson. He was intimately conversant with the history and philosophy of our government. His political views were broad and sagacious. Already some of his political prophecies have become history. Many years ago he predicted the present rebellion as the inevitable result of aristocratic institutions. He brought the light of a clear intelligence to the elucidation of every public question. His large historic reading furnished him with precedents and principles for present guidance. Though a man of intense feelings, he generally subjected his ardor to the restraints of judgment. His feelings were the executive of his reason. He advocated strongly because he saw clearly and felt deeply. He was an ardent partisan—but only in the higher import of the term.

Some men are conservative from mere facility of disposition, or indifference to the public welfare; but Mr. Hoyt was radical from the warmth of his temperament and his vital interest in every question affecting the national well-being. He saw that systems of policy could be carried into execution only through the instrumentality of parties, and that unity and energy of action are essential to political success. Guided by this philosophy, he took sides with all the ardor of his nature. He was, however, superior to party attachments. No political subserviency ever led him to sacrifice his personal independence to love of party; and no false consistency, which under changing conditions exacts unchanging devotion, ever restrained his political freedom. I believe he would have instantly renounced his connection with any party that proved faithless to its principles.

In the Constitutional Convention, Mr. Hoyt soon asserted his native prominence. He spoke on questions of constitutional reform with a practical ability, a breadth of view, and a clear perception of the remote consequences of untried measures, that proved his natural fitness for public pursuits. The Professor,

untrained to political warfare, met in equal battle
champions disciplined by a lifetime of political experience.   He had encounters with ex-Governor
Steele and Franklin Pierce, but his friends were partial enough to think that his gallantry in debate did
not suffer vanquishment in these forensic tournaments.

After the annexation of Texas, Professor Hoyt
spoke often and wrote largely on political subjects.
But his political discussions were mainly limited to
the moral bearings of public measures. The rank and
rapid growth of political profligacy and of irreverence
for constitutional obligations, awakened in him a profound solicitude for the welfare of our country.   He
delivered indignant philippics against corruption in
high places, and strove, by the most vigorous exertion
of tongue and pen, to arrest the course of public im-
morality. Editors, committees, politicians, and leaders
of conventions were constantly availing themselves
of his able pen to draft resolutions and addresses, to
frame political measures, and to define the policy of
his party. Many a weighty paper upon grave political topics which was supposed to emanate from other
sources, really originated in the thoughtful brain of
the Exeter Professor. The influence of his articles
upon the yeomanry of New Hampshire was marked
and salutary. A statesman, eminent in the public
service, assures me that the writings and speeches of
Professor Hoyt did much to revolutionize the politics
of the State, and that for vigor, cogency of logic, and
purity of patriotism, they take equal rank with the
productions of our best political writers.

Chancellor Hoyt was an ardent patriot. Every

chord of his being was attuned to the "music of the Union." His loyalty was based upon the broadest principles of civil ethics. His patriotism, enlightened by historic examples and by profound reflection upon the working of political institutions, was of the heroic stamp. Sam Adams had not a sterner sense of political duty. His devotion to the Union rested upon a clear perception of the sanctity of the oath of allegiance, of the incomparable excellence of our polity, and of the supreme necessity of *one* government to the prosperity of the country. He thought that under existing conditions a conquest of peace could alone furnish a permanent cure of present disorders. He regarded any hope of public welfare in a dissevered Union as fatally illusive, and considered the temporary cessation of hostilities which would spring from a dismemberment of our Republic as only the prelude to a still bloodier drama. He believed that the integrity and supremacy of the Union were essential conditions of enduring peace. In his political creed patriotism was akin to piety, and the civil duties we owe the beneficent Union which has blessed us with constitutional liberty and untold material wealth, were only second in sanctity to our religious obligations.

Mr. Hoyt's career in St. Louis is well known to this community. His appointment as Chancellor of Washington University, the fears expressed by those ignorant of his powers that he might not prove adequate to the responsible duties of his position, the profound impression produced by his inaugural, the ease and skill with which he reorganized the University, his salutary influence upon the young men under his charge, the ability of his public lectures, the attractions of character with which he magnetized strangers into friends, his brave resistance to the forces of disease, his surrender of life, at first reluctant, as if the work of life were not done, at last resigned in Christian submission to the divine will,— these are the pleasing and tearful incidents of his brief Western history. It was fortunate for the fame of Mr. Hoyt that he was the first Chancellor of Washington University. He was placed at the head of the institution during its formative period, and under conditions favorable to the exercise of his great organizing and executive powers. The institution which he found an academy he left a university. Probably no man will ever again in its history effect so wide a change. An enterprise, everywhere arduous, was here made peculiarly difficult by the habits of Western life. The young men of the West are impatient of the restraints of studious life, and anxious to enter upon the active employments of business. Western youth do not generally believe that the study of the classics, or of the higher mathematics, is conducive to their success in life. But happiness and usefulness are the grand ends of life, and what more contributes to human enjoyment and utility than the cultivated tastes and resources of literature and science? How many of the battles of armies and logicians might have been avoided, if the combatants had understood the secret force and nice distinctions of words! The study of language is the investigation of the latent import and structural relations of words—of the philosophy of speech; while the study of mathematics is a scientific examination of the laws and numerical conditions under which the operations of nature are conducted. He is a bold man who will venture to assert that a knowledge of the natural sciences—which explain the phenomena of universe—and of language—which determines the offices of words and the laws of human thought—is unimportant to the well-being of society. The thoughts of retired scholars have again and again revolutionized the commerce of the world, and created arts and trades which have blessed mankind with prosperity and increase of happiness. The commercial and industrial world is not sufficiently sensible of its obligations to learning. The power of careful investigation and of disciplined thought which habits of study cultivate, is capable of transfer and of application to whatever profession the scholar adopts.

These simple truths, which I have interrupted my line of thought to suggest, are generally ignored by Western students. They forget that they reject the highest elements of practical success and refined enjoyment. But, at all events, this eagerness of scholars to leave the halls of learning for the duties of active life, was one of the most formidable obstacles the Chancellor had to encounter in his efforts to establish the University.

Another embarrassment was the immaturity of the students. A university cannot be made of mere lads. The studies of a university course require for their mastery the maturity of an adult understanding. This difficulty arose partly from the reluctance of young men to spend their time in literary pursuits, and partly from the location of the University in the city. The students of country colleges are generally older than those of city colleges. The unwillingness of parents to subject themselves to the expense, or their sons to the temptations, of city life, is a sufficient explanation of this fact. But whatever the cause, the unwelcome fact was not the less a stubborn difficulty, which the success of the University required the Chancellor to overcome. Is it overstepping the modesty of truth to say that he succeeded? By speech and pen, and the influence of his own example, he did much to correct the false views of education which the youth of St. Louis entertained. He reorganized the institution, and infused his own system and scholarship into every department. The obstacles which he surmounted were sufficient to deter men of less dauntless purpose from the undertaking. But he succeeded in organizing an institution which he fondly hoped would be the permanent seat of sound scholarship, polite learning, and Christian culture. The gratitude of this community is due to Chancellor Hoyt for his important services in behalf of Western education.

From the cradle to the grave, Mr. Hoyt enjoyed a degree of popularity and affection which only the most happily constituted natures can ever secure.

When in college, some of the members of his division used to go to him, with a regularity that amounted to a habit, to get him to translate their difficult passages and solve their hard problems. Their expectation of help was never disappointed. He aided them with a cheerful readiness which never paused to think that this generous assistance, which consumed many valuable hours of study and placed inferior minds upon a comparative equality, might injure his rank in the estimation of the Faculty. The moral heroism which saved the life of a student at the imminent risk of his own, the physical courage which taught the college bully a painful lesson of civility, and the kindness which was willing, at any sacrifice of time, to interrupt the most exigent engagements in order to help duller or less industrious students, enthroned him high in the affections of his classmates.

In the society of which he was a member, the political discussions were often violent and stormy. In the parliament of the Brothers in Unity, the debates were at times scarcely less exciting and angry than those which shook the halls of Congress and agitated the nation. Mr. Hoyt mingled in these discussions, which occasionally became fiercely sectional, with a display of forensic ability and a fearlessness in the utterance of his sentiments, that commanded the respect of both parties. On one occasion, the debate terminated in a personal encounter between a Northern and a Southern student. Mr. Hoyt was chosen by the Southron to bear to his antagonist the olive-branch of reconciliation. This friendly office of mediator was peculiarly grateful to his feelings. Pages of general delineation would not show so plainly as this agreeable incident, the estimation in which his candor and good nature were held by his classmates.

In the relation of instructor, strong feelings of personal friendship always subsisted between him and the students under his charge. I have never known a teacher who, without courting popularity, was equally able to secure the personal affections of his scholars. An utter hate of shams; a desire to be taken for just what he was; the entire absence from his nature of anything like deceit; his large powers and attainments; his faithful and learned instruction; the wise and kindly advice which always convinced his students that their teacher was their friend, are qualities that never failed to endear him to his classes.

And in his general intercourse with the world, a marked degree of public favor always attended him. His lectures were universally popular. The press treated him with a courtesy prompted by respect for his character. If criticisms were aimed at his political views, the edge was blunted by expressions of personal regard. His powers of genial and brilliant conversation made him the delight of the social circle. Through all the letters which Mr. Hoyt received from his friends, there breathes a common sentiment of strong and sincere affection.

It requires no careful analysis of Chancellor Hoyt's character to determine the elements of his popularity. The qualities which insured it are at once apparent. His genial nature, his singular simplicity and transparency of character, his cordiality unalloyed with hypocrisy, and his native strength, in which there was no element of pretension, secured for him general esteem and friendship.

Chancellor Hoyt hated pretense with the intensity of Carlyle. From the very depths of his soul he detested every form of deceit and insincerity. His own nature, pure beyond suspicion, was

"Too conscious of right for endurance of wrong."

His indignation kindled over even the fictions of
hypocrisy, and burned with generous heat at the
reality.

A clear head and a good heart are always valid
titles to our respect and affection. 'It was upon these
traits of character that Chancellor Hoyt's popularity
rested.

Chancellor Hoyt loved the "luxury of doing good."
He was the warm friend of indigent merit. His heart
was always touched at the sight of penniless and un-
friended genius. Girard once said he pitied a poor
woman fifteen dollars. Mr. Hoyt's friendship was of
the same practical character. Many a noble youth,
oppressed with the burden of poverty, was enabled by
his generosity to continue his studies. Among the
graduates of Exeter, there are many who are largely
indebted to Professor Hoyt for their opportunities of
culture. In his last sickness, he often sent the luxu-
ries intended for himself to the tables of the destitute,
and gave material aid to loyal men whom the ravages
of civil war had despoiled of their property. Limited
means did not deprive him of the virtue of generosity.
Benevolence is not to be estimated by the magnitude
of the gift. Few men were more liberal, in proportion
to their resources, than Mr. Hoyt. He loved to set
smiles where fortune had placed frowns—to erase
from care-worn brows the "crooked autograph" of
misery, and inscribe instead the smiling signatures
of happiness.

One of the grandest elements in Chancellor Hoyt's

character was a large-hearted humanity. The circumstances of his early life were humble. He worked on the farm till he was eighteen. He was a laboring man all his years. He knew the feelings and wants of the toiling masses. He believed in the dignity of labor. He sympathized with working men. He thought the residence of virtue was in the hearts of the yeomanry, and in their hands the destinies of the country. Labor, the general necessity of the race, he regarded as the prime, Heaven-ordained condition of intellectual growth, social progress, and public virtue. Hence he looked with utter abhorrence upon all institutions which tend to breed a contempt for labor, and to establish an aristocracy of idle wealth and political corruption. That famous line, in which Terence expressed his sympathy with the whole brotherhood of man, was with Chancellor Hoyt a living sentiment, inwrought into the very texture of his being, and pervading, with its fine humanity, the conduct of his daily life. He rested his principles upon the foundations of eternal right, well knowing that the agitations of transient passion and prosperous crime could not shake them. His philosophy contemplated not the aggrandizement of guilty patricians, but the welfare of the race; and not alone the issues of the present hour, but the interests of future generations.

The religious views of Chancellor Hoyt were broad and tolerant, and based upon a careful study of the Scriptures. He had read the New Testament several times in the original, and amended translations which he deemed incorrect. He knew by heart all those passages which theologians quote in support of par-

ticular creeds. His faith was not circumscribed by
the narrow bounds of a sectarian ritual. He always
considered honest and enlightened convictions, however different from his own, entitled to respect. He
thought that diversity of belief was the natural result
of education, temperament, and organization. While,
therefore, he was inflexible in his own views of religious duty, he was tolerant of all honest difference of
opinion. He believed that the Divine Mind accepted
the homage of every devout heart under whatever
peculiarities of form that worship was offered. His
liberal theology did not permit him to think that all
without the pale of his own denomination were guilty
of fatal error. He thought that organic differences
necessarily led to various conceptions of moral obligations and to diverse systems of worship. The qualities of the Divine character which he loved to dwell
upon were justice, love, and mercy. When Mr. Hoyt
was in college, an incident occurred which seriously
modified his spiritual views. In a written discussion,
assigned by the Faculty, it fell to his lot to maintain
the affirmative of the question, "Is the soul material?"
The careful preparation which he made for this debate strongly drew his attention to the corporeal
modifications of the spirit. He observed the influence
which food, climate, and physiological peculiarities
exert over man's spiritual nature, and was led to at-
tribute too great a dependence of spiritual phenomena
upon material conditions. Mr. Hoyt was never, at
any period of life, a materialist. The gross doctrines
which regard the soul as a mere condition of matter
were repugnant to his philosophy. He conceived of

4

the human spirit as essentially distinct from matter, and endowed with a life which the death of the body could not destroy. But a belief in the immortality of the soul is incompatible with the cheerless theories of materialism. Mr. Hoyt's mistake consisted solely in ascribing to man's physical constitution an excessive influence over his spiritual nature. But, at worst, his error was only an exaggeration of physical and psychological truths which we all admit. The calmer judgment of mature years corrected the errors of early days, and gave a truer conception of man's spiritual life. I do not think that Mr. Hoyt's nature was richly endowed with the feeling of reverence. But he who considers a want of veneration inconsistent with a firm belief in the existence of a creative intelligence, has never thought soundly on the phenomena of mind. Reverence springs from the feelings, but belief in the existence of a Supreme Being is the deduction of the reason. The one is emotional, the other intellectual, and there is no logical and constant relation between them. To Mr. Hoyt's love of wit and controversy, to his hate of affectation and hypocrisy, to that candor which freely spoke the thoughts most men would conceal, is doubtless to be ascribed much that bore the semblance of irreverence. In the presence of these great, overshadowing traits, even large veneration would appear small. Beside the Alps, common mountains lose their grandeur. I have no doubt that Mr. Hoyt's excessive desire to avoid every appearance and suspicion of cant led him to do injustice to his religious feelings. Besides, we ought not to estimate a man's spiritual character by

unconsidered expressions uttered in moments of gayety
and social dispute, but by the sober judgments formed
by mature reflection.

Mr. Hoyt's mental constitution and professional
studies led him to prefer the exact sciences. His
mind, by nature and habit, sought to *demonstrate*
every truth. As a scholar, he relied more upon logic
than upon faith. Speculations, unsusceptible of proof,
were distasteful to his mathematical intellect. And
if, in the years of health, and even in the earlier
periods of his illness, he carried this spirit of philo-
sophic inquiry into matters of religion, it ought to ex-
cite no surprise. Is it strange that a man should use the
strongest powers God has given him? Is it wonderful
that a nature essentially mathematical should seek to
prove its priceless hopes? No scientific doubts ever
shook Chancellor Hoyt's faith in a Divine Being. He
only sought to establish his belief by positive evidence.
His clear intelligence recognized the logical necessity
of a prime cause. Years ago he wrote, " I never entertained an unbelieving doubt of the divine authority
and transforming efficacy of the Christian religion."
As he drew near the dark veil which curtains from
mortal view the mysteries of eternal life, he was led,
by solemn meditations upon religious subjects, to repose with a more unquestioning trust upon the conso-
lations of faith. In a late interview, while he already
stood upon the threshold of eternity and was about
to pass into the inner courts of the temple of life, he
expressed, with impressive earnestness, his firm belief
in the great truths of our religion. While he dis-
coursed upon these sacred themes, his eye kindled, his

pale cheek flushed, and his voice rose from feeble whispers to almost its wonted fullness. It seemed as though his face was lighted up with the radiance of immortal hopes. His words, uttered in full view of the solemn realities of another life amid which he was soon to stand, appeared like the dying eloquence of a Christian Socrates. He closed a long conversation upon man's spiritual nature and destiny with these words: "I die a believer in the Christian religion. The three cardinal points of my faith are a belief in a living God—in distinction from an abstract law—in the immortality of the human soul, and in man's personal accountability to his Maker. I have tried to lead a pure life, and to serve God by benefiting man. 'He that loveth not his brother whom he hath seen, how can he love God whom he hath not seen?'

"I do not agree with that ancient definition of eternal life which restricted the intelligence of the soul to a mere consciousness of its experiences in this world, nor do I adopt the Platonic conception of a spirit emanating from the Deity and absorbed again at death into the Divine nature; but I do believe in an active, individual, progressive life after death. God's existence and man's immortality are the twin pillars of our faith—these are the great central facts from which all the other truths of our Christianity are derived. Religion is a many-voiced psalm of thanksgiving—the anthem of a pious life in adoration of our Heavenly Father."

A few days before his death, and at his request, the holy sacrament was administered to him in the presence of his family. He died in communion with the Trinitarian Congregational Church, of which he had been a member for thirty years.

The students of the University will learn with sad satisfaction the affectionate interest the dying Chancellor took in their welfare. His classes never ceased to be the objects of his tender solicitude. He spoke with evident gratification of the kindly relations which had always existed between him and the students, and dwelt with pleasure upon the cordiality with which the members of the institution had co-operated with him in his efforts for their advancement. He was anxious to the last to ascertain the standing and relative progress of the students. In his last hours he summoned some of the students to his bedside, invoked the blessing of Heaven upon them, and bade them a solemn farewell. His desire still to preside over the destinies of the University was one of the strongest causes of his attachment to life. With hopeful augury he predicted for Washington University a career of illustrious usefulness. Even in the unquiet slumbers which brought occasional relief from suffering, his mind revisited the classic scenes, and again solved for the perplexed student the problems of language.

In the illusive health of dreams he rejoiced in the recovery which enabled him to return to pleasant duties, and again provide for the well-being of the University. In one of these restless reveries he imagined himself at the University engaged in the conduct of his recitation, and remarked to his class, "Well, students, I am ready." These words may well express a higher thought—the serene resignation which succeeded his early unwillingness to leave the great enterprises of life unfinished.

The students of the University may borrow from the Chancellor's character valuable lessons for their own direction. Emulating his noble manhood and Christian culture, they will remember that talent without nurture is insufficient, that the hunger of genius must be fed by the strengthening nutriment of labor, and that scholarly excellence is secondary to manly virtue.

Chancellor Hoyt manifested great discretion and delicate tact in his official intercourse with associate teachers. He often said that the Faculty of an institution should be a unit, acting in harmony for the accomplishment of a common result; and he secured this result by a wise management which compelled approval, and by a sympathetic co-operation which made his colleagues his personal friends. His sagacity and his enthusiasm inspired them with one spirit and a common aim. No teacher ever applied to him for counsel or redress in vain. No instructor ever complained to him of any violation of discipline without the offender having immediate occasion to regret the commission of the offense. Nothing provoked him to sterner rebuke than the presumption of a student to disregard the authority of a subordinate teacher. This hearty support of fellow-officers, together with his straightforward dealing and genial intercourse, always bound them to him with feelings of grateful attachment. But the Chancellor thought the obligation of gratitude rested upon himself. He often expressed his sense of great obligation to the Professors of the University for their friendly and efficient co-operation.

He was also deeply mindful of his indebtedness to the Board of Directors, and recalled with frequent acknowledgments their many proofs of personal kindness, their munificent liberality to the University, and their hearty support of his measures and policy.

In his latest hours, when the pallor of death was already on his brow, Chancellor Hoyt spoke with heartfelt emotion of the kindness of his St. Louis friends. In feeble and broken whispers, he regretted his inability to express for himself his deep sense of obligation. He proved himself worthy of favors by his grateful appreciation of them.

During his residence in this city, his independent manhood and frankness of character secured him many friends; and through all the months of his protracted illness, these admirers, whom the nobility of his nature had won, omitted no act of delicate and kindly attention. Though his family ministered to his wants with untiring solicitude, and though his wife, with a devotion that forgot fatigue and courted self-sacrifice in the service of affection, strove to anticipate every wish and to assuage every pang, yet his friends, unwilling to be deprived of this opportunity of showing their sense of his worth, were unremitting in tributes of generous civility. While still able to seek recreation in the open air, carriages were placed at his disposal. When no longer strong enough to leave his room, rich flowers, from friendly hands, shed their fragrance in the sick-chamber. Rare and costly medicines were brought from foreign lands to alleviate his sufferings. Delicacies from many a home gratified every mood of appetite. Graceful tokens of remembrance were sent to him from scenes of festivity, to show that even in hours of gayety he was not forgotten. And finally, this community honored his literary productions with a generous patronage. I have no doubt that these gentle offices, unsought but grateful, smoothed the painful pathway he was treading. Friendship soothed, with its tender services, the anguish of his sick-bed; and sympathy encouraged him, by tokens of affectionate regard, to believe that there were those who were not insensible of his worth nor indifferent to his fate.

For all these delicate courtesies. for all these ministries of kindness, I tender to the friends of Chancellor Hoyt his dying acknowledgments of gratitude.

Only those who have known the privilege and pleasure of Chancellor Hoyt's intimacy can fully appreciate his character or deplore his loss. My pen falters in the narrative of our personal relations. With eyes dim with emotion, I look back through the pleasant vistas of our friendship. Long years ago, as a student of Phillips' Exeter Academy, I became acquainted with Mr. Hoyt. I remember, as though it were yesterday, his first salutation. The words of that kind greeting linger, like music, in the memory of the heart. Stimulated by his friendly encouragements, I gained new hopes of victory in the battle of life, and fresh determination to redress the wrongs of fortune. The friendship which began between the humble pupil and the warm-hearted teacher has never known a moment's interruption. It would require an eloquent gratitude to recount all his kind-nesses. His personal interest, his wise advice, his latchless hospitality, his quick sympathy and cheerful encouragement in moments when life looked sunless, are titles to my grateful regard, which Lethe shall not make me forget. Mr. Hoyt was by no means ex-empt from the imperfections of our frail humanity; he undoubtedly had his faults; but we gladly forget his few defects in the memory of his many excellences.

We mourn a public loss. Chancellor Hoyt fell in the pride of his powers. Had his life been prolonged to the bourn of divine allotment, I feel sure he would have left behind him still greater and more enduring monuments of public usefulness. He was ambitious to leave a memory which good men might cherish, and a fame illustrious for public service. In his last days, Chancellor Hoyt dwelt, with eloquent regrets, upon the incompletion of his plans and labors. He spoke of his schemes for the advancement of the Uni-versity, of the literary enterprises he had projected, and of the lively interest he felt in the educational prosperity of St. Louis and the West. The unre-served consecration of his great powers to the cause of education, and his success in his brief administra-tion of Washington University, justified expectations of wide and eminent usefulness. But that career of honorable service is ended. That Christian manhood, that common sense enriched with liberal discipline, that noble independence of the accidents of fortune, that proud irreverence for titled folly, that lofty scorn for every shape of meanness, that instant sympathy with human suffering, that native affinity with ex-alted natures, that ardent and steadfast friendship is now but a recollection and an influence. The noble example is left, the loved exemplar is gone. The charms which rendered his society so delightful but deepen the sorrows of our bereavement. Bereft of his genial presence, we feel oppressed with a sense of solitude. Death has painfully revealed to us the magnitude of our loss. The gloom of the cypress has succeeded the sunlight of friendship. We stand, chill and desolate, in the shadow of a great grief.

Who could witness, without emotion, the moral grandeur of the death-scene? The soul, weaned from the love of life by the discipline of suffering, and quickened by disease to almost spiritual intelligence, seemed already radiant with light from beyond the grave. The well-ordered household, the affections living in death and surviving its tortures, the impressive exhortations to religious life, the tearful farewell to the members of his family, the soul conscious in dissolution of its immortality and sustained by an unfaltering trust, repeated the solemn triumph of Addison's death, and again showed the sublime fortitude of the dying Christian.

We shall cherish the sacred flame of his remembrance with vestal piety, and seek guidance from the fragrant grave of buried friendship.

> "Thus his memory, like some holy light,
>   Kept alive in our hearts, will improve them,
> For worth shall look fairer, and truth more bright,
>   When we think how he lived but to love them.
> And as fresher flowers the sod perfume,
>   Where buried saints are lying,
> So our hearts shall borrow a sweet'ning bloom
>   From the image he left there in dying."

NOTE.

At a meeting of the Faculty of Washington University, on the morning of Chancellor Hoyt's decease, the following resolutions were adopted:—

Resolved, That in the removal of the late Chancellor Hoyt, by death, we deeply mourn the loss of a wise counselor, a generous colleague, and a peerless teacher.

Resolved, That we share the profound sorrow of his bereaved family, and tender to them our heartfelt condolence at their irreparable loss, commending them to the care of Him who has promised His special favor to the fatherless and the widow.

The students of the University also met, and unanimously

Resolved, That the death of Chancellor Hoyt has deprived us of an able instructor, a kind guardian, and a genial friend.

Resolved, That, in this hour of severe and solemn affliction, we tender to the mourning family the solace of our sympathy, and that we deplore, with a grief akin to their own, the death of our beloved Chancellor.

And on a subsequent occasion, the Board of Directors testified their sense of the loss the University had sustained in the death of its Chancellor, by the adoption of the following preamble and resolutions:—

WHEREAS, It has pleased Almighty God to remove from our midst the late Chancellor of Washington University, Joseph G. Hoyt, while in the prime of life and the ripe and vigorous exercise of his rare powers; and

WHEREAS, It is fitting that the records of this institution bear testimony as well to the eminent merits of the departed—its first Chancellor—as to their earnest appreciation by those to whom its welfare is committed; be it therefore

Resolved, 1st. That the Directors of Washington University deeply deplore the loss which this institution and the cause of edu-

cation has sustained in the death of Chancellor Hoyt. Gifted with
a mind of unusual vigor and clearness, enriched by ripe scholarship
and varied culture, he united to these a temper so genial, so fearless, and so just, and a judgment so mature as to combine, in rare
measure, the talent of felicitous instruction with that of successful
administration. To his unwearied and cordial devotion to its
interests, and his quick and clear perception of its needs, is largely
due the success which the University has thus far attained; and
whatever measure of usefulness may in the future attend its career,
the Directors deeply feel that upon all that future will be impressed
the stamp of his character and his labor.

2d. That to his bereaved family the Directors tender the heartfelt tribute of their sympathy under their heavy affliction.

3d. That in perpetual memory of Chancellor Hoyt, and of the
signal ability with which he discharged its duties, the Professorial
chair in the University heretofore filled by him be henceforward
styled the *Hoyt Professorship of Greek Literature.*

4th. That these resolutions be entered upon the records of the
corporation, and that a copy be sent to the family of the late
Chancellor.

On the morning of the funeral, the Students and
Directors of the University, wearing badges of mourning, escorted the body to the First Trinitarian Congregational Church, where the funeral services were
performed by the Reverend Doctors Post and Eliot.
A plaintive melody, sung by the University Choir,
added, with its solemn and touching strains, to the
impressiveness of the occasion. The procession then
moved to the river, where the students bade adieu to
the form of their beloved Chancellor.

The body was carried to Exeter, New Hampshire,
and there, after piety had performed the final obse-
quies and friendship offered its last homage, it was
laid in a retired and beautiful spot, which years ago
Mr. Hoyt selected as his long resting-place.